The wine sparkled in his eyes and the bells jingled.

My own fancy grew warm with the Medoc.

THE CASK OF AMONTILLADO

EDGAR ALLAN POE

ILLUSTRATED BY GARY KELLEY

CREATIVE EDUCATION

THE CASK OF AMONTILLADO

The thousand injuries of Fortunato I had borne as I best could, but when he ventured upon insult, I vowed revenge. You, who so well know the nature of my soul, will not suppose, however, that I gave utterance to a threat. At length I would be avenged; this was a point definitely settled—but the very definitiveness with which it was resolved precluded the idea of risk. I must not only punish but punish with impunity. A wrong is unredressed when retribution overtakes its redresser. It is equally unredressed when the avenger fails to make himself felt as such to him who has done the wrong.

It must be understood that neither by word nor deed had I given Fortunato cause to doubt my good will. I continued, as was my wont, to smile in his face, and he did not perceive that my smile now was at the thought of his immolation.

He had a weak point—this Fortunato—although in other regards he was a man to be respected and even feared. He prided himself on his connoisseurship in wine. Few Italians have the true virtuoso spirit. For the most part their enthusiasm is adopted to suit the time and opportunity, to practice imposture upon the British and Austrian millionaires. In painting and gemmary, Fortunato, like his countrymen, was a quack, but in the matter of old wines he was sincere. In this respect I did not differ from him materially; I was skillful in the Italian vintages myself, and bought largely whenever I could.

It was about dusk, one evening during the supreme madness of the carnival season, that I encountered my friend. He accosted me with excessive warmth, for he had been drinking much. The man wore motley. He had on a tight-fitting parti-striped dress, and his head was surmounted by the conical cap and bells. I was so pleased to see him that I thought I should never have done wringing his hand.

I said to him: "My dear Fortunato, you are luckily met. How remarkably well you are looking today. But I have received a pipe of what passes for Amontillado, and I have my doubts."

"How?" said he, "Amontillado? A pipe? Impossible! And in the middle of the carnival!"

"I have my doubts," I replied; "and I was silly enough to pay the full Amontillado price without consulting you in the matter. You were not to be found, and I was fearful of losing a bargain."

"Amontillado!"

"I have my doubts."

"Amontillado!"

"And I must satisfy them."

"Amontillado!"

"As you are engaged, I am on my way to Luchresi. If any one has a critical turn, it is he. He will tell me—"

"Luchresi cannot tell Amontillado from Sherry."

"And yet some fools will have it that his taste is a match for your own."

"Come, let us go."

"Whither?"

"To your vaults."

"My friend, no. I will not impose upon your good nature. I perceive you have an engagement. Luchresi—"

"I have no engagement—come."

"My friend, no. It is not the engagement, but the severe cold with which I perceive you are afflicted. The vaults are insufferably damp. They

are encrusted with nitre."

"Let us go, nevertheless. The cold is merely nothing. Amontillado!

You have been imposed upon. And as for Luchresi, he cannot distinguish

Sherry from Amontillado."

Thus speaking, Fortunato possessed himself of my arm, and put-

ting on a mask of black silk and drawing a *roquelaure* closely about my

person, I suffered him to hurry me to my palazzo.

There were no attendants at home; they had absconded to make

merry in honor of the time. I had told them that I should not return until

the morning, and had given them explicit orders not to stir from the

house. These orders were sufficient, I well knew, to ensure their immedi-

ate disappearance, one and all, as soon as my back was turned.

I took from their sconces two flambeaux, and giving one to

Fortunato, bowed him through several suites of rooms to the archway that

led into the vaults. I passed down a long and winding staircase, request-

ing him to be cautious as he followed. We came at length to the foot of

the descent, and stood together on the damp ground of the catacombs of the Montresors.

The gait of my friend was unsteady, and the bells upon his cap jingled as he strode.

"The pipe," he said.

"It is farther on," said I; "but observe the white web-work which gleams from these cavern walls."

He turned towards me, and looked into my eyes with two filmy orbs that distilled the rheum of intoxication.

"Nitre?" he asked, at length.

"Nitre," I replied. "How long have you had that cough?"

"Ugh! ugh! ugh!—ugh! ugh! ugh!—ugh! ugh! ugh!—ugh! ugh! ugh!—ugh! ugh! ugh!"

My poor friend found it impossible to reply for many minutes.

"It is nothing," he said, at last.

"Come," I said, with decision, "we will go back; your health is precious. You are rich, respected, admired, beloved; you are happy, as once I was. You are a man to be missed. For me it is no matter. We will go back; you will be ill, and I cannot be responsible. Besides, there is Luchresi—"

"Enough," he said; "the cough is a mere nothing; it will not kill me. I shall not die of a cough."

"True—true," I replied; "and, indeed, I had no intention of alarming you unnecessarily—but you should use all proper precaution. A draught of this Medoc will defend us from the damps."

Here I knocked off the neck of a bottle which I drew from a long row of its fellows that lay upon the mould.

"Drink," I said, presenting him the wine.

He raised it to his lips with a leer. He paused and nodded to me familiarly, while his bells jingled.

"I drink," he said, "to the buried that repose around us."

"And I to your long life."

He again took my arm, and we proceeded.

"These vaults," he said, "are extensive."

"The Montresors," I replied, "were a great and numerous family."

"I forget your arms."

"A huge human foot d'or, in a field azure; the foot crushes a serpent rampant whose fangs are embedded in the heel."

"And the motto?"

"Nemo me impune lacessit."

"Good!" he said.

The wine sparkled in his eyes and the bells jingled. My own fancy grew warm with the Medoc. We had passed through long walls of piled skeletons, with casks and puncheons intermingling, into the inmost recesses of the catacombs. I paused again, and this time I made bold to seize Fortunato by an arm above the elbow.

"The nitre!" I said; "see, it increases. It hangs like moss upon the vaults. We are below the river's bed. The drops of moisture trickle among the bones. Come, we will go back ere it is too late. Your cough—"

"It is nothing," he said; "let us go on. But first, another draught of the Medoc."

I broke and reached him a flagon of De Grâve. He emptied it at a breath. His eyes flashed with a fierce light. He laughed and threw the bottle upwards with a gesticulation I did not understand.

I looked at him in surprise. He repeated the movement—a grotesque one.

"You do not comprehend?" he said.

"Not I," I replied.

"Then you are not of the brotherhood."

"How?"

"You are not of the masons."

"Yes, yes," I said; "yes, yes."

"You? Impossible! A mason?"

"A mason," I replied.

"A sign," he said.

"It is this," I answered, producing from beneath the folds of my *roquelaure* a trowel.

"You jest," he exclaimed, recoiling a few paces. "But let us proceed to the Amontillado."

"Be it so," I said, replacing the tool beneath the cloak and again offering him my arm. He leaned upon it heavily. We continued our route in search of the Amontillado. We passed through a range of low arches, descended, passed on, and descending again, arrived at a deep crypt, in which the foulness of the air caused our flambeaux rather to

glow than flame.

At the most remote end of the crypt there appeared another less spacious. Its walls had been lined with human remains, piled to the vault overhead, in the fashion of the great catacombs of Paris. Three sides of this interior crypt were still ornamented in this manner. From the fourth side the bones had been thrown down, and lay promiscuously upon the earth, forming at one point a mound of some size. Within the wall thus exposed by the displacing of the bones, we perceived a still interior crypt or recess, in depth about four feet, in width three, in height six or seven. It seemed to have been constructed for no especial use within itself, but formed merely the interval between two of the colossal supports of the roof of the catacombs, and was backed by one of their circumscribing walls of solid granite.

It was in vain that Fortunato, uplifting his dull torch, endeavored to pry into the depth of the recess. Its termination the feeble light did not enable us to see.

"Proceed," I said; "herein is the Amontillado. As for Luchresi—"

"He is an ignoramus," interrupted my friend, as he stepped unsteadily forward, while I followed immediately at his heels. In an instant he had reached the extremity of the niche, and finding his progress arrested by the rock, stood stupidly bewildered. A moment more and I had fettered him to the granite. In its surface were two iron staples, distant from each other about two feet, horizontally. From one of these depended a short chain, from the other a padlock. Throwing the links about his waist, it was but the work of a few seconds to secure it. He was too much astounded to resist. Withdrawing the key I stepped back from the recess.

"Pass your hand," I said, "over the wall; you cannot help feeling the nitre. Indeed it is *very* damp. Once more let me *implore* you to return. No? Then I must positively leave you. But I must first render you all the little attentions in my power."

"The Amontillado!" ejaculated my friend, not yet recovered from his astonishment.

"True," I replied; "the Amontillado."

As I said these words I busied myself among the pile of bones of which I have before spoken. Throwing them aside, I soon uncovered a quantity of building stone and mortar. With these materials and with the aid of my trowel, I began vigorously to wall up the entrance of the niche.

I had scarcely laid the first tier of the masonry when I discovered that the intoxication of Fortunato had in a great measure worn off. The earliest indication I had of this was a low moaning cry from the depth of the recess. It was *not* the cry of a drunken man. There was then a long and obstinate silence. I laid the second tier, and the third, and the fourth; and then I heard the furious vibrations of the chain. The noise lasted for several minutes, during which, that I might hearken to it with the more satisfaction, I ceased my labors and sat down upon the bones. When at last the clanking subsided, I resumed the trowel, and finished without interruption the fifth, the sixth, and the seventh tier. The wall was now nearly upon a level with my breast. I again paused, and holding the flambeaux over the mason-work, threw a few feeble rays upon the figure within.

A succession of loud and shrill screams, bursting suddenly from the throat of the chained form, seemed to thrust me violently back. For a brief moment I hesitated, I trembled. Unsheathing my rapier, I began to grope with it about the recess; but the thought of an instant reassured me. I placed my hand upon the solid fabric of the catacombs, and felt satisfied. I reapproached the wall; I replied to the yells of him who clamored. I re-echoed, I aided, I surpassed them in volume and in strength. I did this, and the clamorer grew still.

It was now midnight, and my task was drawing to a close. I had completed the eighth, the ninth, and the tenth tier. I had finished a portion of the last and the eleventh; there remained but a single stone to be fitted and plastered in. I struggled with its weight; I placed it partially in its destined position. But now there came from out the niche a low laugh

that erected the hairs upon my head. It was succeeded by a sad voice, which I had difficulty in recognizing as that of the noble Fortunato. The voice said:

"Ha! ha! ha!—he! he! he!—a very good joke indeed—an excellent jest. We will have many a rich laugh about it at the palazzo—he! he! he!—over our wine—he! he! he!"

"The Amontillado!" I said.

"He! he! he!—he! he! he!—yes, the Amontillado. But is it not getting late? Will not they be awaiting us at the palazzo, the Lady Fortunato and the rest? Let us be gone."

"Yes," I said, "let us be gone."

"*For the love of God, Montresor!*"

"Yes," I said, "for the love of God!"

But to these words I hearkened in vain for a reply. I grew impatient. I called aloud—

"Fortunato!"

No answer. I called again—

"Fortunato!"

No answer still. I thrust a torch through the remaining aperture and let it fall within. There came forth in return only a jingling of the bells. My heart grew sick; it was the dampness of the catacombs that made it so. I hastened to make an end of my labor. I forced the last stone into its position; I plastered it up. Against the new masonry I re-erected the old rampart of bones. For the half of a century no mortal has disturbed them. *In pace requiescat!*

A CLOSER LOOK

Mysterious and suspense-filled, "The Cask of Amontillado" was first published in the magazine *Godey's Lady's Book* in November 1846 and is a prime example of Edgar Allan Poe's Gothic sensibilities. Poe's masterful use of irony and an eerie first-person narrative combine to evoke a sense of horror in the reader. That a man with no clear motive could commit the perfect crime, living with his actions without apparent remorse and without detection, is a psychological feat that is unattainable by characters in Poe's other Gothic tales.

By telling the story from the murderer Montresor's coldhearted point of view, Poe presents Montresor's calculating methods as a rational outcome of "the thousand injuries" committed by his "friend" Fortunato (7). However, Poe soon directs the reader to question Montresor's claims, especially after mentioning his vengeful family motto *"Nemo me impune lacessit"* ("No one offends me unpunished"). This character is not meant to be an object of sympathy—if anyone deserves sympathy, it is the story's unfortunate victim, Fortunato.

Although Montresor's objective is to punish Fortunato for the man's betrayal, his vengeance is devoid of meaning because Fortunato has no idea what he has done. He is an unwitting victim. By smiling and repeatedly calling Fortunato "my friend," Montresor engages Fortunato's compliance in their quest for the amontillado, but Fortunato does not realize that this search is merely a ruse and that Montresor is not a well-meaning friend. Montresor, who is also consumed by the act of revenge, has failed to achieve his goals by his very definition of what "successful" revenge entails: "A wrong is unredressed when retribution overtakes its redresser. It is equally unredressed when the avenger fails to make himself felt as such to him who has done the wrong" (7). But the murderer is unaware of his failure, it seems. By using such examples of dramatic irony, in which the reader knows more about something than a character in the story does, Poe takes a simple tale of murderous revenge and makes it into something more menacing and intricate.

This was not a typical Gothic tale for Poe's day and age. The historical Goths were a Germanic people who lived in northern Europe; to the cultured Greco-Romans in the south, they seemed dark and bar-

barous. Their tribal name came to be associated with architectural and literary styles that deviated from the norm and were shadowy or somewhat frightening. The basic Gothic literary plot came to involve a vicious pursuit of an innocent victim for purposes of gaining some form of power, which took place in an eerie setting. Such tales of horror were popular in the 19th century, and Poe's dark personality made him particularly suited to the genre. He brought in a psychological element that makes his brand of Gothicism all the more horrifying—and personal—because it addresses the issues of a tortured mind.

Montresor preys on Fortunato's egotism to lure him away from the pre-Lenten festivities of the "carnival season"; knowing how conceited Fortunato is about wine, Montresor tells him that he needs his help discerning whether or not he has made a wise purchase of some amontillado. Amontillado is a special variety of sherry, and it takes a true wine connoisseur to distinguish between it and any other sherry, something that Fortunato is certain the person named Luchresi cannot do justly. Once he has baited him, Montresor makes it impossible for Fortunato to refuse. Fortunato is psychologically trapped before he has even entered the catacombs. Not being the one to "help" Montresor would insult Fortunato's pride and reputation, two things that this man seems to value above all else.

Montresor pushes Fortunato into the ready-made cell both physically, by taking Fortunato by the arm as they enter the innermost catacombs (13), and verbally, by invoking Luchresi's supposed expertise for the fourth time (16). When he has been secured to the granite wall, Fortunato still has no clue what is going on (16–17), just as he was unaware of what the Montresor family arms were (12). The testing of the amontillado is finally proven to be a ruse, but the jester Fortunato fails to understand that the joke is on him until it is much too late. Once he has literally sealed Fortunato's fate, Montresor begins to feel the pangs of regret, but he attributes it to the surroundings instead and refuses to blame himself for his own actions (21). Even though he does not admit his guilt, he will live with it silently. His conscience will not "rest in peace," for vengeance is always a crime. And he has committed the worst crime against himself, depriving himself of his humanity by heartlessly killing another. He cannot feel the damp chill of the catacombs. He cannot feel the beating of his cold, dead heart. That heart will remain buried with his other victim for the next 50 years.

ABOUT THE AUTHOR

Edgar Allan Poe was born January 19, 1809, in Boston, Massachusetts. His parents, both actors, would have only a shadowy role in his young life; his father abandoned his wife and three children when Poe was two years old, and his mother died soon after. Raised by foster parents John and Frances Allan in Richmond, Virginia, and in England, Poe continued his education at the University of Virginia in 1826. He dropped out during his first year, though, as his studies had been replaced by excessive drinking and gambling. The young Poe was handsome, charming, and withdrawn—but when he drank, his personality became volatile.

Following a disagreement with John Allan, Poe returned to Boston, where he anonymously published his first collection of poems, *Tamerlane and Other Poems*, in 1827. He then enlisted in the United States Army for a short time and was discharged in 1829. Jobless and destitute once again, Poe sought out a widowed aunt, Maria Clemm, in Baltimore, Maryland, and moved in with her family. Mrs. Clemm had taken in Poe's older brother Henry as well, and the siblings were reunited for a short time. In

Edgar Allan Poe

Baltimore, Poe published his second book of verse while waiting to begin his appointment at West Point Military Academy.

Life at West Point was not to Poe's liking, however; within six months, he was habitually skipping classes and the required church services to provoke the school into dismissing him. He succeeded. Poe returned to Baltimore and the Clemms, where he began to pursue a literary career in earnest. In the early 1830s, Poe turned to writing short stories, publishing several and gaining enough recognition to earn a job as an assistant editor at the *Southern Literary Messenger*. His problem with alcoholism was his greatest impediment, though; Poe was fired after spending only a few weeks at the *Messenger* but was allowed to return after he pledged to be on his best behavior. As an editor, he had the opportunity to have many of his own stories, poems, and critical reviews published, and his growing reputation soon helped increase the journal's circulation.

In 1836, the 27-year-old Poe married his 13-year-old cousin Virginia Clemm. The couple was relatively poor but happy, and the loving support of both Virginia and her mother, Maria, was beneficial to a man disposed to heavy drinking and bouts of severe melancholy. Alcohol and depression constantly caused Poe professional and personal grief. Not until the late 1830s was he able to sustain work and start to produce some of his best mature writing. His book *Tales of the Grotesque and Arabesque* was published in 1839 and was later heralded as one of the most important works in American literature. Poe became widely known for his macabre, death-ridden themes and fantastic, mythic tales. These tales, set in dark, foreboding atmospheres and usually centered on a horrible mystery, came to exemplify the Gothic style.

After Virginia developed tuberculosis in 1842 and began a slow spiral toward death, Poe turned ever more to alcohol and writing to escape his pain and fears. He composed some of his most haunting and disturbing stories during this period, including "The Tell-Tale Heart" and "The Pit and the Pendulum." In 1845, he published "The Raven," a wildly popular poem, and the next year brought "The Cask of Amontillado," his most critically acclaimed tale. Poe was a fast writer, but he took care to complete all his projects. He once said, "The true genius shudders at incompleteness— and usually prefers silence to saying something which is not everything it should be." But no matter how well his work was received or which critic hailed him as a genius, it never translated into monetary success for Poe.

Poe attempted to form relationships with other women after Virginia passed away in 1847, but his unhealthy and unshakeable habits invariably disrupted the romances, and Poe spent the last two years of his life battling his personal demons. He died on October 7, 1849, after collapsing in the streets of Baltimore. Since any official records have long been lost, the true cause of Poe's death is unknown. However, many speculative theories have persisted, including that he had been drunk and beaten; he had contracted rabies; or that he had been afflicted with cholera, a deadly bacterial disease that was common at the time.

Despite his difficult, undistinguished life, Poe had a remarkable and lasting effect on subsequent authors and thinkers—especially outside America, where translators made Poe more accessible in their native tongues. From French poet Charles Baudelaire to British critic W. H. Auden to Russian novelist Fyodor Dostoyevsky, many people around the world extolled the virtues and influence of Edgar Allan Poe, the master of the macabre.

Published by Creative Education

P.O. Box 227, Mankato, Minnesota 56002

Creative Education is an imprint of The Creative Company.

Design by Rita Marshall; production by Heidi Thompson

Page 22–30 text by Kate Riggs

Printed in the United States of America

Library of Congress Cataloging-in-Publication Data

Poe, Edgar Allan, 1809–1849.

The cask of amontillado / by Edgar Allan Poe.

p. cm. – (Creative short stories)

ISBN 978-1-58341-580-1

1. Revenge—Fiction. I. Title. II. Series.

PS2618.C373 2008

813'.3–dc22   2007008482

First edition

2 4 6 8 9 7 5 3 1